One Wordy Bird

Pets at Work
PAW PALS

studio fun
INTERNATIONAL

Studio Fun International
An imprint of Printers Row Publishing Group
A division of Readerlink Distribution Services, LLC
10350 Barnes Canyon Road, Suite 100, San Diego, CA 92121
www.studiofun.com

Getty Photo Credits: P.114: zabelin/gettyimages.com,
P.116-117: cynoclub/gettyimages.com, P.118: Denja1/gettyimages.com,
P.119: Thomas Demarczyk/gettyimages.com,
P.120-121: LuckyBusiness/gettyimages.com
P. 122-123: ScoobyDoo2/gettyimages.com

Written by Brenda Scott Royce
Illustrated by Colleen Madden
Designed by Candace Warren

Printers Row Publishing Group is a division of
Readerlink Distribution Services, LLC.
Studio Fun International is a registered trademark of
Readerlink Distribution Services, LLC. All rights reserved.

All notations of errors or omissions should be addressed to
Studio Fun International, Editorial Department, at the above address.

ISBN 978-0-7944-4109-8
Manufactured, printed, and assembled in Guangzhou, China.
First printing, January 2019. GD/01/19
23 22 21 20 19 1 2 3 4 5

Library of Congress Cataloging-in-Publication Data is available on request.

5-7% of the purchase price will be donated to
The American Society for the Prevention of Cruelty to Animals® (ASPCA®),
with a minimum donation of $50,000 through December 2019.

For Susie, a fellow lover of
birds and books.
—B.S.R.

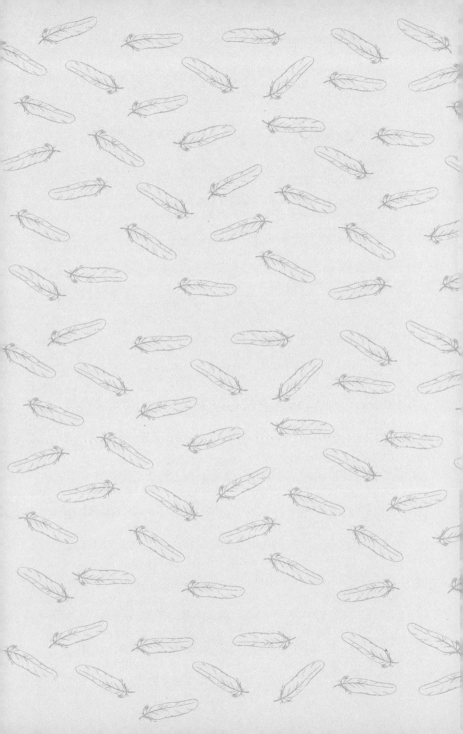

1

A New Assignment

A sign posted outside the library read NO ANIMALS ALLOWED. Meg Harper was about to enter the building when she saw the sign and stopped short. Stepping to one side of the door, she signaled the black and white dog at her side to sit. When he did as instructed, she patted his head and said, "Good boy, Chance." Then she gave him a treat from the small pouch she always carried when they were out together.

Meg's cousin Amanda Midori caught up to them a moment later. In contrast to Meg's relaxed attire—jeans and a plaid shirt with rolled-up sleeves—Amanda looked positively professional. She wore a black skirt with a lavender blouse and had a large presentation board tucked under one arm. She balanced a tray of cookies in both hands.

Meg pointed at the sign, and Amanda shrugged. "It's okay. Chance is a certified service dog. Besides, he's the star of the show."

"It's not a show," Meg protested.

"It's an educational demonstration, a.k.a., a show," Amanda said. "I should know, since I'm the one who booked it."

The library appearance was the first event Amanda had organized as part of Project PAW, which the two cousins had started along with their friends Drew Bixby and Blanca Montez. The goal of the project was to spread the word about the amazing abilities of working animals—including Chance, who'd been trained to help Meg cope with her epilepsy. She'd been diagnosed with this disorder, which caused her to have periodic seizures, when she was about six years old. Chance had come to live with her recently, after she and Amanda found him abandoned in front of Amanda's parents' animal grooming salon.

Meg looked back toward the parking lot. "Where's Aunt Becky?"

"She said to go ahead without her. She'll be in as soon as she gets Willow dressed again." Amanda's little sister had a crazy habit of pulling off her clothes during car rides. The library was only a few blocks from the Midori's house, but the toddler had managed to take off her shoes, socks, and most of her shirt along the way. "Can you get the door?" Amanda said. "My hands are full."

Meg reached for the door, then hesitated, pointing at another sign. This one read NO FOOD ALLOWED.

"Yeesh, Meg, you worry too much," Amanda said. "I discussed everything with the librarian last week. He knows we're bringing snacks. Now, let's get inside or we'll be late."

⎯⎯⎯⎯ ⇒ ⎯⎯⎯⎯

Amanda was pleased with the turnout. Not counting her mother, who sat in the back row with Willow in case her little sister got cranky (or decided to disrobe), there were about twenty people gathered in the library's reading room. Some had come specifically for the event; others ambled in after seeing the presentation board Amanda had set up on an easel near the entrance.

The board read MEET CHANCE, SUPER-HERO SERVICE DOG in bold, glittery letters, and then, in a smaller font: PRESENTED BY PROJECT PAW (PETS AT WORK). Underneath the text, Amanda had pasted photos of Chance in his official red vest, including one of him and Meg graduating from the training program they'd both had to pass in order for Chance to become a certified service animal.

The librarian, Mr. Henderson, introduced them, then Amanda went to the podium. Even though Chance was Meg's dog, they'd planned the presentation so that Amanda would do most of the talking. Meg tended to get tongue-tied around strangers, and besides, she needed to keep her attention focused on Chance to make sure the dog didn't get stressed or overexcited being around so many people.

Amanda didn't mind being in the spotlight one bit. Standing up straight, she began: "Chance is a border collie, a breed known for being intelligent and hardworking. As you may know, border collies are often

used by farmers to help herd sheep. Chance has a different job. He's a seizure-response dog, or seizure dog for short. A seizure dog goes through special training to help someone with epilepsy."

"Eppaweppy!" Willow shouted from the back row. Amanda was embarrassed by her little sister's outburst, but several audience members giggled. She waited for the laughter to die down before continuing.

The presentation concluded with Meg guiding Chance through some of the behaviors he had been trained to perform— summoning help, pressing an alarm button, offering comfort, and providing physical stimulation in the event Meg became woozy or lost consciousness. Chance performed to perfection, and Amanda thought everyone in the audience seemed very impressed.

Several people approached them afterward with questions. Others wanted their picture taken with Chance. As the last of the guests filed out of the reading room, the librarian approached Amanda. "Your mother wanted me to tell you that she took your little sister to the kids' section and that you should meet her there when you're ready to leave."

Amanda nodded. "Would you like us to stack the chairs or put the tables back to the usual arrangement?"

"No, thank you," Mr. Henderson replied. "We're having a poetry reading here tonight, so the chairs and podium are fine just the way they are." To Meg, he added, "I didn't see your parents. Did they come today?"

Meg shook her head. "They don't like to watch me have seizures—even when it's make-believe—and I'd have been even more nervous if they were in the audience, so I came with my Aunt Becky." Chance stood by her side, tail wagging as she spoke.

"This guy certainly looks happy," Mr. Henderson said. "May I pet him?"

"Thanks for asking," Meg said. "Yes, you may. When the presentation ended, I gave him an 'off-duty' signal. That lets him know it's okay for him to relax, play, or interact with people. He especially enjoys the people part."

"Chance is a real 'people dog'!" Amanda added.

The librarian leaned over and gave Chance a good scratch behind the ears. "You were terrific," he told the dog. Then he straightened and said, "All three of you did a great job. I think people learned a lot about service animals."

Amanda nodded in agreement. "Most people have heard of seeing-eye dogs, but they don't realize that there are lots of different types of working animals."

"I read an article recently about dogs who act as 'reading buddies' at schools and libraries," the librarian said. "Kids who have difficulty reading often improve their skills by reading aloud to animals."

"Dogs don't judge," Meg said matter-of-factly. "They're good listeners, too.

It makes sense that they can help kids be better readers." She looked down at her dog and patted his head lovingly. "I wonder if Chance would make a good reading buddy?"

"Chance already has a job," Amanda reminded her. "But we could find another dog for the library. Maybe that could be Project PAW's next assignment!" Her brown eyes sparkled with excitement as she looked up at the librarian.

Mr. Henderson stroked his chin as he considered the suggestion. Finally, he said, "If a library dog can help children improve their reading skills, then it's sure worth a try. Especially if you can find one as sweet and well-behaved as Chance!"

2
Amanda's Plan

"Next time maybe Willow can stay home," Amanda told her mother as they walked to the library parking lot. "I was so embarrassed when she shouted in the middle of the show!"

"It was a *presentation*, not a show," Meg said again. "And I thought it was funny. I wasn't embarrassed, and I'm the one with 'eppaweppy.'"

Willow looked up at Meg from her stroller and laughed.

Mrs. Midori clicked her key fob to deactivate the car's alarm. "At least Willow kept her clothes on!"

Amanda was putting the presentation supplies into the trunk of the car when she saw a white pick-up truck slide into a nearby parking space. She recognized the vehicle even before she saw her friend Blanca climb out of the passenger seat. "It's Blanca and Mrs. Montez," Amanda called to her mother. "Can we go say hi?"

Mrs. Midori was lifting Willow into her car seat. "Yes, just be quick. Tell Mrs. Montez I said hello."

Blanca grinned when she saw Amanda and Meg approaching with Chance. "Sorry I couldn't come for the presentation," she told them. "I had to wait for my mom to get off work. How did it go?"

"Great!" Amanda told Blanca about the event and their conversation with Mr. Henderson afterward. "We're going to try to find a dog who'd make a good reading buddy for the library."

Blanca bounced up and down with excitement. "That's a great idea!"

Mrs. Montez greeted the girls with hugs. "Are you staying for the poetry reading?" She held up a bright yellow flyer advertising the event. At the center of the flyer was a photo of a serious looking man with a gray beard and round glasses.

Amanda shook her head. She wasn't crazy about poetry—and even if she wanted to attend, it wouldn't be a good idea to bring her baby sister. "We have to get Willow home, and I still have Saturday chores."

"And I need to feed and walk Chance." Meg gestured at the flyer. "Is that the poet? He looks familiar. Will he be here?"

Blanca's face fell. "He died last month. Tonight's event is a celebration of his life and his work. He lived around here, so lots of people in town knew him."

"Maybe you saw the article in yesterday's paper," Mrs. Montez told Meg. "'Local poet leaves rare book collection to library.'"

"The article said he had thousands of books in his house," Blanca added. "Can you imagine? I love books so much! I wish I had thousands of them."

"Then where would we keep your stuffed animals and all the other things you love so much?" Mrs. Montez gave her daughter an affectionate pinch on the cheek. "We should get inside."

———— ⇛ ————

Amanda stifled a yawn. It was Monday morning and she'd stayed up late the night before researching animal reading buddies. She found an article online that confirmed what Mr. Henderson had told them— that reading aloud to dogs can improve children's literacy skills. Her excitement grew as she learned that reading buddy programs can also have positive effects on the animals who participate. By the time she finally went to bed—two hours past her bedtime—she'd printed several articles and prepared a plan of action.

Now, sitting on the front stoop of her neighbor Drew Bixby's apartment building, she held a stack of four presentation binders with the Project PAW logo on the cover. *They look professional*, she thought with pride. She knew she sometimes went overboard with stuff like this, but she couldn't help it. She enjoyed making reports and presentations for school, and now that she and her friends had started Project PAW, she wanted to use those skills to help animals.

When Drew emerged from his building, backpack slung over one shoulder, she handed him one of the binders.

"What's this?" he asked.

"It's our first official assignment," she announced. "We're going to help Mr. Henderson find a dog to be a reading buddy at the library." As they walked the four blocks to school, Amanda filled him in on her conversation with the librarian. "Do you still volunteer at the Grant County Animal Shelter?" she asked him.

"I go there on Saturdays," he said, bobbing his head. "I have almost enough hours to earn my Wildlife Wings." Drew belonged to the Ready Rangers, a local scouting group. Of all the activities he'd participated in through the program, helping out at the animal shelter had been his favorite.

"Good," Amanda said. "Next time you're

there, see if any of the dogs might make a good reading buddy."

Drew cast a sideways glance at Amanda. "How am I supposed to do that?"

She smiled and pointed at the presentation binder he'd tucked under one arm. "I researched what makes a good animal reading buddy. I also made a list of dog breeds that have been used as reading buddies at different schools and libraries. It's all in the prospectus." Amanda liked the word *prospectus*. It sounded more professional than *report*.

"Prospectus?" Drew rolled his eyes. "Since I started hanging out with you, Amanda, I feel like I'm in business school instead of the third grade."

Even though she wasn't sure he meant it as a compliment, Amanda was flattered. She dreamed of starting her own business one day. "Thank you."

3

At the Shelter

Most kids his age wouldn't think of helping the other shelter volunteers clean kennels as a fun way to spend a Saturday morning, but Drew didn't mind doing dirty work—especially if it meant being around animals. He liked all animals, but dogs were his favorite, so he was especially happy when he was assigned to the canine wing—like today. A few other Ready Rangers were also earning their Wildlife Wings by volunteering at the shelter. On Saturdays, Drew's father or one of the other troop leaders drove them and stayed to supervise the Rangers while they worked at the shelter. Today, Mr. Bixby was using his handyman skills to build a large perch for a recently arrived macaw named Maxine.

"Watch out, Dad, Maxine is a flirt," Drew warned his father when he stopped by the shelter's office to get more cleaning supplies. The large blue-and-yellow macaw had been at the shelter for just a few weeks, but she'd already gained a reputation. Drew had learned that macaws are very sociable birds. The shelter's director, Mrs. Noland, had decided to keep Maxine's cage in the shelter's office so that she'd be around a lot of people. Drew had noticed the bird liked to be the center of attention. Whenever anyone talked to her, she bobbed her head and made happy chattering sounds. But when she was left alone, she'd call out loudly, "Helllllooooooo!"

Mr. Bixby laughed as he drilled holes into a large wooden rod. "I think I can handle a flirty bird."

Returning to the dog wing, Drew thought about Amanda's request that he help find a dog that could become a reading buddy for the library. He'd read her "prospectus," so he knew that the best dogs for the job are calm, patient, and attentive. Golden retrievers and Bassett hounds topped Amanda's list of possible breeds, but there were none of those currently at the shelter.

"Hello, pal." Drew knelt beside a kennel where a dachshund named Stryker was curled on a cushion. At the sound of Drew's voice, Stryker hopped up. The little dog yapped as he jumped and twirled in circles. "You're a hyper hotdog," Drew said, smiling down at the dog. Stryker was friendly, but Drew feared his perky personality might not be the best fit for library visits, so he moved down the row.

A half hour later, Drew had found the dog whose personality, in his opinion, best fit

Amanda's criteria. It was a schnauzer named Arnie. "You're a mellow fellow," Drew told Arnie after talking to him for a while. Mostly gray with a white beard, the dog sat calmly staring up at Drew while he spoke. At least, Drew believed he was staring at him—it was hard to tell with so much hair hanging in the dog's eyes!

A shelter worker named Chad told Drew that Arnie had arrived in terrible condition— filthy, matted, and covered with fleas. The dog had been bathed and treated with flea medicine but still looked pitiful. The poor creature looked like he'd walked through a car wash and dried off in a wind tunnel. Despite his sweet temper, Drew didn't think kids would want to cuddle up and read with Arnie.

He considered asking Mrs. Noland her opinion about Arnie but decided to talk to Amanda first. She was the project's leader, after all. If she thought Arnie was suited to library service, they could come to the shelter together to discuss the idea with Mrs. Noland.

When his volunteer shift was over, Drew found his father in the office, putting the finishing touches on Maxine's perch. It looked more like a treehouse, actually—with multiple branches for climbing and round hooks for hanging bells and bird toys. A braided rope ladder connected a lower resting platform to a higher one. The macaw was climbing up the ladder, using her beak like a third foot to grasp the rope, when Mrs. Noland entered the office.

"It's marvelous!" she exclaimed, admiring Mr. Bixby's craftsmanship. "Now she won't have to stay in her cage all day."

Drew wondered why they'd gone to the trouble of building such an elaborate structure for an animal who would most likely be adopted soon. Maxine was a beautiful bird—with brilliant blue top feathers, a golden chest, and a touch of green on her forehead. She was smart, too. Although "hello" was clearly her favorite, she could say about a dozen words. Who wouldn't want a pet like her? He posed the question to Mrs. Noland.

The shelter director tucked a strand of silver hair behind one ear. "I'm afraid it's much trickier to find a home for a macaw than it is for a dog or a cat. They demand a lot of time and attention, and they can be loud and destructive. And because they can live up to fifty years, many—like Maxine—outlive their owners. Adopting a macaw is a big commitment, and it's not right for everyone."

"Fifty years?" Drew said, amazed. "How old is she now?"

"About fifteen or sixteen," Mrs. Noland responded. "So she still has a long life ahead of her." Patting his back, she added, "Don't worry, Drew. We'll find Maxine a good home, but it may take a while. In the meantime, she'll have plenty of people to interact with in the office—and a wonderful climbing structure to explore! I can't thank you enough, Mr. Bixby."

"My pleasure." Drew's father smiled and put a hand on his shoulder. "Come on, Drew. Let's round up the other Rangers and head home."

Drew said goodbye to Mrs. Noland and Maxine. "Bye-bye," the bird said in a sing-songy voice. "Come back sooooooon!"

4

A Big Offer

"Hey!" Amanda looked up from her science textbook. She and Meg were doing their homework in the dining room of Amanda's apartment over WASH AND WAG, the Midori family's grooming salon. Meg spent most afternoons at Amanda's until one of her parents got off work and came to pick her up. "Number eight is about us!"

"*Us?*" Meg said, her tone conveying both disbelief and frustration. "Slow down.

I'm only on number five."

"Cousins," Amanda clarified. They'd just begun studying genes in science class. Amanda loved learning how physical traits like eye color and height are determined by DNA. She knew she got half her DNA from her mother and half from her father. She had black hair and brown eyes like her father, and was tall like her mother. But she never would have imagined she shared any genes with her cousin. Indeed, besides their love of animals, she and Meg were nothing alike.

Amanda had super-straight black hair; Meg's was light brown and wavy. Even though she was the younger of the two cousins, Amanda was taller by a few inches. Meg struggled with math and science—

Amanda's best subjects. Meg did better in history and geography, perhaps because she'd traveled a lot with her family. Amanda's parents ran their own business and rarely took time off for vacations. Though her father had been born in Japan, Amanda had never been there. Meg, meanwhile, had lived in Tokyo for a few months and could even speak a little Japanese.

"Question eight," Amanda said, reading aloud from her homework. "What fraction represents the genetic similarity between first cousins?"

Meg looked up, her forehead wrinkled in concentration. "Our mothers are sisters, so that makes us first cousins. Siblings usually share one-half of the same DNA. That means cousins..." After a moment, she shook her head. "I have no idea."

They heard footsteps climbing the stairs from the grooming salon below, then a voice called out, "Hello?"

"It's Drew," Meg said as their friend reached the top step.

He waved at the girls and told Amanda, "Your mom said I could come up."

Amanda nodded. "Where were you after school? We walked home without you."

Drew pointed to the green and white jersey he wore. "Soccer practice. Season just started. I can't walk home with you guys on Mondays or Wednesdays for a while."

"We'll survive," Amanda teased,

motioning for Drew to join them at the dining room table. While he waited for them to finish their homework, he ate some apple slices from a snack plate Amanda's mother had prepared for them.

"Found it!" Meg said, pointing at a page in her science text. "According to this family tree chart, first cousins have about one-eighth of the same DNA."

Amanda looked at the chart. She would never have guessed that she and Meg had one-eighth of anything in common, but she wrote down the answer and moved on to the next question.

When they'd finished their work, Drew told them about the shelter dogs, especially Arnie the shaggy schnauzer. "He's the calmest, coolest dog there," he concluded. "But with his crazy cyclone hair, he doesn't look like a dog you'd want to bring to the library."

"We could brush him," Meg suggested.

"That dog needs more than a hairbrush," Drew said with a chuckle. "He needs a lawn mower."

Amanda slapped one hand on the table, like she often did when she had an idea. "My parents can groom him!"

Drew looked thoughtful. "That would be awesome, but how will we get him to the salon?"

"They have a mobile grooming van. They can drive it to the shelter and groom Arnie in the back. I'll bet there are other dogs there that need to be groomed, too."

"Definitely yes." Drew nodded. "There are some real scruffballs. They get baths, but lots of them need their hair and nails trimmed, too."

"What about cats?" Meg wondered.

"Cats, too." Amanda stood, her excitement mounting. "They'll groom all the animals— at no charge!"

———— ⇒ ————

Later, after Drew and Meg had left, Amanda helped her parents close up the salon. Amanda's older brother Gage was upstairs playing video games and keeping an eye on Willow. As she mopped the floor, Amanda told her parents about her plan. She thought they'd be as enthusiastic as she

was to help Arnie and the other shelter animals. When both stopped their work and stood staring at her she realized she'd miscalculated.

Her mother shook her head. "You shouldn't have done that, Amanda."

"No," her father added in a stern voice. "Not without asking us first."

Amanda bit her lip and blinked back tears. She hated disappointing her parents. "I'm sorry. I got so excited, I didn't stop to think—"

"We'd love to help, sweetheart," Mr. Midori said, placing a hand on Amanda's shoulder. "But we're way too busy. It's hard enough taking care of you kids and running this salon. We just don't have the time to groom a shelter full of animals."

Amanda stared down at the floor. "I understand." Looking up at them, she added, "Can I go make a phone call? I need to ask Drew not to talk to Mrs. Noland about my offer."

When Drew answered the phone, his voice was bubbling with excitement. "I called the shelter," he said. "You should have heard Mrs. Noland's voice when I told her the news. Free grooming for every animal in the shelter!"

"Oh, no." A sick feeling rose in Amanda's stomach. She was too late.

5

Down in the Dumps

The fact that it was Taco Tuesday at Pinegrove Elementary did little to brighten Amanda's spirits. The school's tacos weren't as good as the ones served at her favorite Mexican restaurant, but she still loved them. Today, though, she had too much on her mind to care about food. As Blanca and Meg devoured their tacos, Amanda picked a tiny piece of chopped tomato off hers and popped it into her mouth.

Blanca eyed Amanda's tray. "Aren't you hungry?"

Meg turned in her seat to stare at her cousin. "You've been acting down in the dumps all morning. What gives? You were so happy yesterday when Drew told us about Arnie."

"Who is Arnie?" Blanca asked.

"He's a schnauzer," Meg responded. "Drew thinks he has the personality—but not the looks—to be a reading buddy at the library. So Amanda had the brilliant idea to have her parents bring their grooming van to the shelter and give him a free makeover! And not just Arnie, but all the animals."

"Brilliant!" Blanca agreed.

Amanda noticed Blanca staring at her

uneaten taco, so she slid it onto her friend's plate. "You can have it. I don't have much of an appetite."

"Thanks," Blanca said. "Wait till we tell Mr. Henderson we've found a dog for his reading program."

"No, we can't tell him." Amanda rubbed her hand over her forehead. "I made a promise I can't keep. My parents can't groom the animals."

Meg frowned. "Not even Arnie?"

Amanda shook her head. "I made the offer without their permission. I should have known better, but I got carried away. Drew already told Mrs. Noland at the shelter about the offer, and she's thrilled about the free grooming. I have to go there today after school and tell her the truth."

"Oh no. I'm sorry, Amanda. I know you didn't mean to cause trouble. And we'll find another dog for the library," Blanca said. "We just have to."

The bell rang and the girls stood and gathered their trays. As they were leaving the cafeteria, Meg told Amanda, "I'll go with you to talk to Mrs. Noland. I got to know her pretty well when I adopted Chance."

Amanda put one hand on her hip and turned to her cousin. "You have to go with me anyway, since we walk home together." In a softer voice she added, "Thank you."

———— ⇒ ————

In Mrs. McKay's English class, the students were reading from *The Island of the*

Blue Dolphins, one of Blanca's favorite books. She'd read it twice before it was assigned to the class. Even though she knew the story inside and out, her heart still raced when the heroine, Karana, jumped off a ship to go back for her brother, who'd been left behind on their island homeland.

A boy named Aaron was reading aloud from his seat in the second row. Aaron had played Ben Franklin in the school play last year and was a good actor. His voice lifted when Karana begged the chief not to set sail without her brother. Blanca hoped when it was her turn that she'd get to read an equally exciting part of the story.

After Aaron had read a few paragraphs, Mrs. McKay called on another student, a girl named Janelle. Blanca sighed, wishing she'd been selected instead. Janelle was not the best reader. Her small voice rarely raised above a whisper, and she often struggled to pronounce longer words. Today, she stumbled over an easy one, "forlorn," saying "floor-lorn." Some of the kids in the back of the classroom giggled at the gaffe.

Janelle stopped reading and looked up at Mrs. McKay. In a trembling voice she said, "I'm sorry. I can't." Squinting, she added, "There's ... something in my eyes, I think."

The teacher tapped Meg to take over reading and asked Janelle if she'd like to visit the school health office. "No, thank you, I'll just rest my eyes for a minute," the girl said, crossing her arms and putting her

head down on her desk.

Meg was a good reader, but Blanca was no longer paying attention to the story. Instead she was thinking of Janelle. The girl never volunteered in class, and when she was called on to read aloud, she often got herself excused, like today.

With or without an audience, Blanca loved to read—so she'd never realized how difficult it could be for some kids. Lately, she'd been reading about library dogs for Project PAW. She'd learned there were lots of different reasons some kids struggled with reading—and most had nothing to do with intelligence. Some had learning disorders such as dyslexia, which made it difficult to interpret words and letters.

Others had speech impediments. A stutter or a lisp could make someone self-conscious. Shy kids might read well in private but freeze in front of a crowd. Then, of course, there were the kids who just plain didn't like to read—as crazy as that seemed to Blanca. She wondered if Janelle fit one of those categories—or if she really did have something in her eyes.

Janelle remained bent over her desk, face buried in her arms, until the bell rang.

Blanca caught up to her as they exited the classroom. "It's a really great story. Karana has to learn to hunt and survive on the island all alone after her brother—" She put a hand over her mouth. "Oops. Spoiler alert!"

"It's okay." Janelle smiled. "I've read the

book. I know what happens."

"Then you *can* read," Blanca blurted. "That's great! I thought you had a learning disability or something. So, why do you always try to get out of reading in class?"

Janelle's mouth dropped open but she didn't speak. Her cheeks reddened.

Blanca immediately regretted her words. She'd been genuinely curious and hadn't meant to embarrass her classmate. Her mother often warned her that her nosiness would get her into trouble. "I'm sorry. I didn't mean—"

Before she could finish her sentence, Janelle took off running. Blanca tried to catch up, but Janelle had already disappeared into the sea of children exiting the school and heading toward the waiting buses.

6

Meeting Arnie

When Amanda opened the front door to the Grant County Animal Shelter, a voice called out. "Helllooo!"

"Hello?" Amanda stepped inside, followed by Meg and Drew. She looked around but didn't see anyone. There was no one at the front desk. She rang a bell on the counter.

"Hellloooo," the voice repeated.

Amanda looked through an open doorway

to the hallway beyond. "Mrs. Noland?"

At the third "hello," Drew broke into a grin and pointed at the large macaw in the corner. Maxine was perched on a curved branch near the top of the climbing structure Mr. Bixby had built. "That's Maxine. She's been here a few weeks. How's the weather, Maxine?"

The macaw cawed, "hot-hot-hot," and the girls laughed.

Just then Letty Noland appeared in the doorway. "Sorry to keep you waiting." Seeing the kids, she said, "Hello, Drew. And Meg Harper, how nice to see you again." She reached over to shake Meg's hand. "How's Chance?"

Meg's border collie had lived at the shelter for a short while after he'd been abandoned by his previous owner. Mrs. Noland had been instrumental in helping Meg and the dog get into a service dog training program at the university. "He's doing fine, thank you," Meg replied. "Do you remember my cousin, Amanda Midori?"

"Yes, of course." The shelter director shook Amanda's hand. "We're all so excited about your family's generous offer to groom all our animals!"

There was an awkward pause as Amanda looked down at the floor, and Drew and Meg exchanged glances. Finally, Amanda lifted her head and spoke. "They can't do it. I'm sorry. I meant it when I made the offer, I really did. But I didn't realize how much work that would be for my parents..."

"I'm disappointed," Mrs. Noland said when Amanda finished telling her story, "but your heart was in the right place." She put an arm around Amanda's shoulder and squeezed gently. "Grooming all the animals in this facility would be a massive under-taking. I should have known it was too good to be true. I appreciate you coming here to talk to me in person. I know you're probably disappointed, too."

Amanda felt pressure lifting from her chest. She'd spent the whole day worrying about how Mrs. Noland would take the news. She was thankful the woman was so understanding. "I really am sorry."

"Sooorrry," Maxine mimicked. The wordy bird brought a smile to Amanda's face.

"Would you like to meet Arnie?" Drew asked Amanda, who nodded eagerly. He turned to Mrs. Noland. "Is it okay if I take them back to the dog wing?"

———— ⇒ ————

"I see what you mean," Amanda told Drew when she got her first glimpse of Arnie the schnauzer. "He's one hairy hound."

Mrs. Noland had escorted the kids to one of the shelter's small "meet-and-greet" rooms, where families could interact with animals they were considering adopting. She'd left them there, and a few minutes later, a worker named Chad arrived with Arnie. When Chad unclipped the dog's leash, Arnie lumbered over to Drew and sniffed at his shoes. Then he plopped down at his feet.

"He is very calm," Meg observed. "He wouldn't frighten little kids, even ones who are nervous around dogs."

"He wouldn't frighten a flea," Chad agreed as he watched the dog's reaction to the kids.

Drew let out a chuckle. "He might frighten himself if he ever looked in a mirror."

Meg sighed. "Poor thing probably can't see himself in a mirror. There's so much hair in his eyes." Leaning down, she smoothed back the thick, tangled hair that covered the dog's forehead.

After spending several minutes with Arnie, Amanda and Meg agreed that Drew was right about the dog. Underneath all that scruff lay a pooch with a sweet personality. Maybe he'd enjoy visiting

schools and libraries and interacting with kids.

"One more thing," Amanda said, removing a book from her backpack. She opened it and began reading aloud. At the sound of her voice, Arnie scooted closer. He lay down next to her and put his head on her lap. Chad's eyebrows raised in surprise. Amanda looked up at her friends and flashed them a big thumbs-up.

By the time the three friends left the shelter, Amanda had come up with another plan. She told Meg and Drew about it as they walked home. When they reached the salon, they found Mr. Midori in the back, trimming a standard poodle. Without waiting for him to finish, Amanda launched into her plea. "Can you please groom one of the shelter dogs, Dad? Just one. Please?" She told him about Arnie's friendly demeanor, and Drew chimed in to say of all the shelter residents, Arnie was the one who would most benefit from a professional grooming. "I'll pay for it with whatever's in my piggybank."

Meg offered to chip in, too. "Please, Uncle Andy. Arnie can help kids overcome reading challenges. He'll be a different kind of therapy dog, kind of like how Chance helps me live with epilepsy." Smiling up at him, she said, "Onegaishimasu." One of a handful of Japanese words she learned while living with her family in Tokyo, it meant *please*.

By the time Mr. Midori used his trimmer to shape the hair on the poodle's tail into a perfect puffball, he'd heard enough. "Okay, okay, I'll do it," he said. "Free of charge. But only if the Paw Pals help."

7

Grooming Days

Amanda's father was the first to call the kids the "Paw Pals," but he wouldn't be the last. Mr. Hook, a teacher who'd gone to Meg and Amanda's library presentation with Chance, passed them in the halls later that week and said, "Look, it's the Paw Pals!" During his volunteer shift at the shelter on Saturday, Drew told Chad about Project PAW. When he was leaving for the day, Chad said to Drew, "Say hi to your Paw Pals for me."

Before long, the name stuck. Amanda decided to make T-shirts with the words PAW PALS on the front and the logo she'd designed with Chance's picture on the back. She hoped to raise the money to get them printed before their next presentation.

It was too bad they couldn't make them in time for today, Amanda thought as she and Meg rode to the shelter in the Wash and Wag mobile grooming van. Amanda was wearing a royal blue jumpsuit with a matching headband and white sandals. Meg, meanwhile, wore cutoffs and an oversized white shirt with both sleeves rolled up to the elbows. Once again Amanda found herself wondering how her DNA and Meg's could be one-eighth the same.

When Mr. Midori pulled the van around to the shelter's back entrance, Drew and Blanca were already waiting to meet them. Drew went inside the shelter and returned moments later with Chad, who was carrying Arnie in his arms.

"Oh, my," Mr. Midori said when he finally got a good look at the mop-haired mess of a dog. "So, this is Arnie?" He took out his smartphone and clicked on the camera app. "I think I'll take before-and-after shots for the salon photo album."

Amanda walked around to the side of the van and slid open the panel door. The interior of the van gleamed in the morning sun. The equipment was similar to what they had at the salon, but adapted to the smaller space.

Chad handed the dog off to Mr. Midori. "I'll be inside if you need anything. Thanks for doing this."

"You're welcome." Mr. Midori lifted Arnie into the van and carried him straight to the large stainless steel tub. "This is going to be a big job," he said to the kids as they got to work.

While Mr. Midori handled most of the actual grooming, the kids helped with shampooing, blow-drying, and combing. Amanda, who was the most familiar with the tools of her father's trade, handed him the supplies he needed. Blanca and Meg massaged medicated lotion onto Arnie's cracked toe pads. Drew's self-appointed task seemed to be cracking jokes and fetching snacks—both for the dog and his handlers.

———— ⇒ ————

The dog that emerged from the van forty minutes later looked nothing like the one who had entered it. Mr. Midori had cut off most of Arnie's matted hair. He kept it long around the face, preserving the schnauzer's trademark beard, which was now nearly white and neatly trimmed. He also clipped the dog's toenails, cleaned his ears, and took a few inches off his bushy eyebrows.

The shelter staff and volunteers on duty that day were all stunned by Arnie's transformation. "Wow," Chad said when Amanda handed him the other end of Arnie's leash. "Dude has eyes, after all!"

As they walked down the hallway to the dog wing, the schnauzer looked all around him as though seeing his surroundings for the first time.

Mrs. Noland met them near Arnie's kennel. "He's adorable," she said with a smile. "I can't believe you did all that in such a short amount of time."

"With so many helpers the work went pretty quickly," Mr. Midori told her. "I'm not due back at the salon for a couple hours, so maybe I could groom some more dogs." Before his daughter could get carried away again, he added, "Just a few."

"That's very generous," said Mrs. Noland.

Amanda kissed her father on the cheek. "Thanks, Dad!"

As Mr. Midori returned to his van to prepare for the next dog, Mrs. Noland turned to Drew. "Why don't you pick out the animals you think are most in need of a makeover. Maybe it will help them get adopted."

"Sure," Drew said. "I have a couple ideas."

Just then a familiar screech echoed down

the halls. "Hello! Helllooooo!"

Mrs. Noland sighed. "I've left Maxine alone too long. She gets lonely, you know." She turned and started down the hall.

Amanda trailed after her, gesturing for the rest of the Paw Pals to follow. "Can we come with you?" she called after the shelter director. "We want to talk to you about Arnie."

———— ⇛ ————

Amanda wished she'd brought her prospectus—or even some of the photos of canine reading buddies that she'd printed from the Internet. Lacking such visual aids, she did her best to summarize the Paw Pals' goal to find a dog who could be a reading buddy for the library.

Sitting behind her desk, Mrs. Noland listened attentively. Maxine the macaw seemed to be listening, too. The big bird bobbed and nodded throughout Amanda's speech. When Amanda finished, Maxine called out, "More!"

"I've heard about animal reading buddies," the shelter director said at last. "And I like the idea of helping Mr. Henderson find one that could make appearances at the library. But there's a lot to consider. First of all, whoever ends up adopting Arnie might not want to participate in the program. Does Mr. Henderson want a dog?"

Amanda shrugged. She hadn't thought to ask him that question. But Blanca spoke up. "I talked to him at the poetry reading.

He said he loves dogs but lives alone and works long hours at the library. He was concerned that he wouldn't have time to train it."

"No, that doesn't sound like an ideal arrangement," Mrs. Noland concurred. She pushed her chair back and stood. "Why don't you work with Arnie while he's still here. There are some books and magazines in the waiting room. You can take turns reading to him, and see how he reacts. Then we'll take it from there."

For the next few hours, the Paw Pals took turns reading to Arnie and helping Mr. Midori. They had selected one cat—a calico, and two dogs—both mutts, for makeovers. All three were vastly improved by their visits to the grooming van.

When Amanda and Blanca arrived at the meet-and-greet room, they found Drew shaking his head in frustration. "He used to lay around like a sweet, shaggy mop," he said, pointing at the schnauzer. "Now he won't stop running around. I think it's the haircut. Now that he can see what's in front of him, he wants to go exploring."

Amanda gestured at the sports magazine in Drew's hands. "Maybe he just doesn't like what you're reading."

"Who doesn't like baseball?" the boy asked. "Besides, Meg read him one of those rhyming books for little kids. He wouldn't sit still for that, either."

"He might enjoy poetry," Blanca said. "I love poetry."

"Good luck finding a book of poetry around here," Drew said.

"I have plenty of poems memorized." Blanca sat cross-legged on the floor and began reciting one of her favorites, a poem about a lonely lion who finally finds a friend.

As Drew and Amanda watched, Arnie circled Blanca and then settled down beside her. Maybe Blanca was right and the dog preferred poetry. Then Arnie put his paws over his ears and let out a mournful howl.

Amanda was crestfallen. It seemed her friends were right. She remembered the qualities of a good reading buddy that she'd listed in her prospectus: calm, patient, and

attentive. The "new and improved" Arnie was none of those things.

The dog had abandoned Blanca's side and was now chewing on a wooden chair leg. As Drew tried to offer Arnie a chew toy to replace the chair, Amanda shook her head sadly. "This dog is not cut out for library life."

8

Finding a Family

Before   After

"Attention!" Amanda lifted a banana from her tray and tapped it on the table in front of her. "I'm calling this meeting to order." She was sitting across from Meg and Blanca at their usual table. Both looked up from their lunch trays expectantly.

Drew rolled his eyes. "This is a cafeteria, not a conference room." He pointed to the fruit in Amanda's hand. "And that's a banana, not a gavel."

Since the third and fourth graders had the same lunch period, Drew sometimes sat with them in the cafeteria—when he wasn't hanging out with his soccer buddies or the members of his comic book club. Today Amanda had insisted he eat with the Paw Pals so they could discuss important business.

"That's a good idea." Amanda set down the banana and picked up a pencil. She made a note on the pad in front of her: "Order a gavel."

"Are we going to start looking for another library dog?" Meg asked. "Is that what this meeting is about?"

Amanda shook her head. She removed a

piece of paper from her folder and placed it on the center of the table. On it she'd printed two pictures of Arnie that she'd downloaded from her father's smartphone. Underneath the images were the words BEFORE and AFTER. The other kids gasped. Though they'd witnessed the dog's transformation in person, seeing the photos side by side still made a big impression.

Seeing that the photos had the effect she'd intended, Amanda began her prepared speech. "I think we gave up on Arnie too soon. I've been thinking about him—and Chance."

Meg perked up at the sound of her dog's name. "What about Chance?"

"Chance needed training to be a seizure

dog, right?"

Meg nodded, remembering all the sessions she and Chance attended at the university—and the hundreds of hours they practiced outside of class. "I still run through his lessons with him, to make sure he doesn't forget."

"I think Arnie can learn to do his job, just like Chance did." She looked around the table at her friends. "We can help him."

"Maybe he needs a test run," Meg suggested. "We could bring him to the library and see how he does."

"I'll ask Mr. Henderson." Blanca grinned, dimples forming in her cheeks. "My mom's taking me to the library today after school. We volunteered to help organize

Cornelius Bryson's books."

Drew wrinkled his nose. "Who's Cornelius Bryson?"

"He's the poet who donated his rare book collection to the library. There are stacks and stacks of boxes! Mr. Henderson said he could really use help unpacking and sorting through all the books."

"I'll go with you," Drew offered. "I don't know much about poetry, but I'm good at unpacking boxes." He reached for the before-and-after photos of Arnie. "Can we bring these pictures to show Mr. Henderson?"

"Good idea," Meg said. "While you two are at the library, Amanda and I can visit the shelter and talk to Mrs. Noland."

"Agreed." Amanda made a final notation

on her pad, then set down her pencil. She picked up the banana and banged it on the tabletop. "Meeting adjourned."

"Lunch period doesn't end for ten more minutes," Drew pointed out.

"I know." Amanda winked as she began peeling the banana. "But I really want to eat this gavel."

Maxine was chattering away when Amanda and Meg arrived at the animal shelter. A family of five was in the front office with Mrs. Noland. The parents were filling out paperwork, and their three children were talking to the macaw. Amanda could tell by the way the bird bobbed her head and fluffed her feathers that she was enjoying the attention. She hoped the family had decided to adopt Maxine.

But when she asked the shelter director, the answer was not what she expected.

"This is the McCarty family," Mrs. Noland said. "They want to adopt Arnie."

Mr. McCarty and the children took Arnie on a walk in the neighborhood around the shelter while Mrs. McCarty finished the adoption paperwork with the shelter staff. Mrs. Noland told the cousins that it was looking like Arnie would be going to a new home that day. "The McCartys have a large property outside of town, with lots of room for a dog to run around. They've got chickens and horses, not to mention the three kids, to keep him busy. Arnie really seemed to like the children. I think it'll be a good fit."

"That's great, but what about our plan for him to be a library dog?" Amanda asked. "Should I talk to the McCartys about Project PAW? I can print them a copy of my prospectus, and—"

"That won't be necessary," Mrs. Noland interrupted gently. "I told them about the reading buddy program, and they said they can't participate. They live too far from town, and they're very busy with their family farm." She reminded the girls that they'd known this was a possibility, and they could still try to find another dog—and another family—to take part in the project.

The director's words made sense, but Amanda still felt terrible. She didn't want to start over with a new dog. She had her heart set on Arnie. One glance at Meg's face told Amanda that her cousin felt the same way. They might not have many of the same genes, but in some ways—like their love of animals—they were exactly alike.

"Can we say good-bye to Arnie?" Meg asked in a shaky voice. "In case we never see him again?"

Mrs. Noland gave the girls a sympathetic smile. "Of course."

"You and your friends really made a difference in Arnie's life," she told them when they reached his kennel. "Since his makeover, we've had several inquiries about him. There was a waiting list to adopt him! That's something you can all be proud of."

Amanda nodded. She was glad their actions had helped Arnie find a loving home, and hoped the other animals they groomed would also get adopted soon. Yet as she walked home with Meg, she couldn't help but feel that their first official assignment had been a failure.

9

A Fitting Tribute

"The Cornelius Bryson Reading Room," Amanda read the gold-plated sign above the entrance to the room where she and Meg had given their presentation a few weeks earlier. Since that time, upon a recommendation from Mr. Henderson, the library's board of directors had voted to rename the room in honor of the beloved local poet. With the help of volunteers, Bryson's sizable book collection had been organized and catalogued. Some of the rarer volumes had been placed in a display case in the reading room, while the rest were shelved throughout the rest of the library. The poetry section alone had tripled in size.

"Looks great, doesn't it?" Blanca said, staring up at the sign. "I was sad when he died, but I'm glad he left his books to the library so that people can enjoy them."

The Paw Pals had come to the library for the dedication ceremony. It seemed to Amanda like half the town was there. Inside the reading room, people milled about, admiring the display and the portrait of Cornelius Bryson that had been framed on the wall. Mrs. Montez, who'd arrived early to help set up for the event, was sitting in the front row, along with Meg's parents.

"Dude had a lot of books," Drew said, exhaling at the memory of all the boxes he'd helped to unload.

"What kinds of books?" Amanda asked. She still wasn't crazy about poetry but loved reading novels and short stories.

"Mostly the heavy kind."

A few minutes before the ceremony was scheduled to begin, Mr. Henderson entered the room and began greeting guests. When he spotted Amanda and her friends, he said, "Hello, Paw Pals. Thanks for coming today. Any progress finding a reading buddy?"

Frowning, Amanda filled him in on recent events. "It's a lot harder than we thought," she concluded. "It's not enough to find the right dog, we also need to find the right owner."

"That's because they need to be a team," Meg added. "Like me and Chance."

The librarian let out a wistful sigh. "Gee, I wish I could have a dog, but like I told Blanca, I don't know that I have the time to train a dog or give it the attention it would need. I have a tiny apartment and spend most of my time here at the library." After glancing at his watch, he thanked the kids for their efforts and made his way to the podium.

———— ⇒ ————

Mr. Henderson welcomed the guests and named all the volunteers who'd helped with the effort to rename and reorganize the reading room—including Drew, Blanca, and Mrs. Montez. Then he turned over the podium to Dr. Lois Hammond, a university professor who'd been a close friend of the poet's.

"Before I talk about my friend Cornelius, I thought I'd read some of his work," the professor said, opening a leather-bound book and setting it on the podium. "He wrote so many wonderful poems, but this is my favorite. It's called, 'One Wordy Bird.'" Dr. Hammond pushed her glasses higher on her nose and began to read.

Amanda had expected to zone out during the poetry portion of the ceremony, but a few phrases—"feathers fair of blue and gold" and "jibber-jabber uncontrolled"—caught her attention. By the end of the first verse, she

was convinced that the bird in the poem was the same one the Paw Pals had befriended at the shelter: Maxine!

She glanced over at her friends. She could tell by their shocked expressions and excited whispers that they'd come to the same conclusion. Of course, she realized now, the macaw had come to live at the shelter right around the time the library received the donation of books. Both had occurred shortly after the newspaper had announced the poet's death.

Amanda wanted to hear the rest of the poem, but she had an idea and could no longer sit still. She whispered something into Meg's ear, then slipped out of her seat and tiptoed from the room.

Amanda was waiting in front of the library when her father pulled up in the Wash and Wag mobile grooming van. Since meeting Arnie, Mr. Midori had decided to donate a few hours each weekend to grooming animals at the shelter. She'd called him from the library, reaching him just as he was packing up the van.

"What's going on?" he asked her when she climbed into the front seat. "I thought you couldn't make it to the shelter today because of the library event. What made you change your mind?"

"A poem," Amanda said, "Crazy, huh? I don't even like poetry." Pointing to the road, she added, "Just drive. I'll explain on the way."

At the shelter, Letty Noland confirmed that Cornelius Bryson was Maxine's original owner. "He had no living relatives, so he left the bird to us, along with a sizable donation for her care. We used some of the money to buy the materials for her perch," she said, gesturing to the fancy climbing structure Drew's father had built. "I heard he also left part of his estate to the library."

"I just came from there." Amanda was still clutching the program from the dedication ceremony. A photo of Cornelius Bryson was printed on the cover. She walked over to the perch and showed it to Maxine. The bird showed no sign of recognition.

The inside of the program included

a few of Bryson's poems, including "One Wordy Bird." Amanda asked Maxine, "Is this about you?" and began reading.

The bird listened attentively, ruffling her feathers and bobbing her head in tune with the poem's meter. "Good, good," she cooed in obvious delight.

Amanda heard the shelter's front door open and looked up to see Meg entering with her parents. "We knew you'd be here," Meg told her cousin. Drew was right behind her, followed by Blanca and Mrs. Montez.

Maxine squawked, "more!" and Amanda realized she'd stopped reading when her friends entered. She finished the poem, then told her friends, "I'm sorry I ran out of the ceremony, but I had an idea."

"I think we all had the same idea," Drew said, speaking for the rest of the Paw Pals. "We were so focused on finding the right dog, we didn't realize that the perfect reading buddy was in front of us the whole time!"

Mrs. Noland clapped her hands together. "I think Mr. Bryson would be very pleased with the idea of Maxine helping children to read. But remember, a service animal is one-half of a team. Who will be Maxine's guardian?"

Amanda looked up at the blue-and-yellow macaw, whose soft chattering seemed to indicate contentment. The bird liked being the center of attention. "I've got a pretty good idea about that, too."

10

Fine-Feathered Friend

Pets at Work
PAW PALS
Amanda
Midori

Helping pets help people!

"Hellllooo," Maxine the macaw greeted the members of Mrs. McKay's fourth grade class. The students responded in unison, "Hello!"

The big blue and yellow bird was perched on the shoulder of her new owner. Amanda, Meg, and Blanca exchanged excited glances as their teacher introduced their special guests.

Mr. Henderson grinned as he gave Maxine a pine nut, one of her favorite treats. Amanda had never seen the librarian so happy.

Several weeks had passed since the Paw Pals had approached him about adopting Maxine. Due to his work schedule and small apartment, the librarian had ruled out owing a dog, but he liked the idea of having a pet macaw—especially one that shared his fondness for literature. He visited the shelter to meet the bird that same day, and soon Maxine had a new home.

Mrs. Noland referred him to an aviculturist—an expert at raising birds— for advice on handling the macaw. He did additional research on his own, reading nearly every book on bird care in the library.

Once he and the bird had bonded, he began bringing Maxine to story time, where she was an instant hit with the kids. The fancy perch Mr. Bixby built for Maxine was moved to the library's reading room. Surrounded by books and the portrait of her original owner, Cornelius Bryson, the bird seemed very much at home during her library visits.

Mr. Henderson also planned to bring the bird to daycare centers, hospitals, and nursing homes—anywhere they could share their love of books and reading with others. Amanda, the self-appointed leader of the Paw Pals, had organized today's visit to Mrs. McKay's class, Maxine's first elementary school appearance.

"Macaws are highly intelligent,"

Mr. Henderson told the kids. He described the species' ability to mimic human speech and showed the newest additions to Maxine's vocal repertoire—"woof" and "meow," which she'd picked up during her stay at the shelter. Then he shared the story of how, thanks to the Paw Pals, he'd come to be Maxine's owner. With a nod to Amanda, he said, "I wanted a reading buddy, and I got a reading *birdy*."

He picked up a book he'd brought with him and held it up for the children to see. "Maxine's original owner used to read to her all the time. When he was working on a new poem, he'd recite it over and over until he was happy with it. I think that's why she's so fond of rhyming books. Her favorite is *Green Eggs and Ham.*" At the sight of the book, Maxine bobbed her head and chirped happily.

"Who would like to read to her first?" the librarian asked.

Hands shot up around the room. Blanca was surprised to see that Janelle, who never liked to read in class, was among the volunteers. "Pick Janelle," she whispered to the librarian, pointing to the girl in the next row.

———— ⇒ ————

Standing in front of the class, Janelle held the book up and read aloud to Maxine. The text was simple but with all eyes on her, the girl seemed understandably nervous. Her hands shook when she turned the page. When she stumbled over a word, she blushed and dropped her head to her chest.

Mrs. McKay stepped forward and put her arm around her student's shoulder. "Thank you, Janelle. Would you like to stop now?"

Before the girl could answer, Maxine squawked, "More, more!"

Janelle looked up at the bird. Maxine stared back at her, head bobbing with anticipation. After a moment, Janelle started reading again, her small voice growing stronger with every stanza. After a few more pages, the librarian thanked Janelle and let another child take a turn at reading to the bird.

As Janelle was making her way down the aisle to return to her seat, Blanca reached up to give her a high-five. "Spoiler alert,"

Blanca whispered. "He really does like green eggs and ham."

Janelle let out a short burst of laughter. "I know how the story ends! I can read, you know."

"Yeah." Blanca smiled and nodded. "I know you can."

The sign outside the library's front entrance had been modified. Under the words NO ANIMALS ALLOWED, Mr. Henderson had added "EXCEPT SERVICE ANIMALS."

Meg stepped to one side of the sign, signaling the border collie beside her to sit. "Good boy, Chance," she said, slipping the dog a treat. Chance's black and white hair gleamed in the morning sun.

"Move a little to the right, please." Tammy Pham, a photographer for the newspaper, gestured to Meg. Then she positioned Mr. Henderson and Maxine on the other side of the sign. "Smile," she urged them, squeezing a squeaky toy in

hopes of getting both dog and bird to also look at the camera. Maxine must have been used to having her photo taken. Unprompted, the bird sang out, "Cheeeese!"

The newspaper was doing a story on working animals, especially the library's new reading buddy. The photographer had already taken a group shot of Maxine and the four Paw Pals. Now they all headed inside, where several children and their parents—including Willow and Mrs. Midori— were awaiting the bird's scheduled appearance at story time.

Amanda had created business cards for the Paw Pals. As they entered the library she handed one to the photographer, along with a list showing the proper spelling of each of their names. "Feel free to e-mail me if you have follow-up questions."

Project PAW's first official assignment was a success, Amanda thought as she watched Maxine interact with the children. The bird was calm, patient, and attentive, just as a reading buddy should be. She'd seen how Maxine was able to get kids excited to read. Now she realized that the activity was just as beneficial for the macaw. At the shelter, she'd been well cared for—but seldom the center of attention. As a library buddy, she'd go on regular outings and meet lots of new people. It was the perfect arrangement for a highly intelligent, social creature.

"Mr. Henderson was right," Amanda told

her friends. "Reading buddies can make a big difference."

"So can we," Meg added, putting one arm around her cousin's shoulder. "Now, what should our next project be?"

A Real-Life Reading Buddy

One Wordy Bird was inspired by the true story of Buddy the macaw. Buddy is registered as a therapy animal with Pet Partners, a Community Partner of the ASPCA.

Buddy and his owner live in Arizona, where they make regular visits to libraries, schools, and nursing homes. Buddy's calm and curious nature make him the perfect reading buddy. He listens closely and nods his head with the turn of each page. Many children return again and again for the chance to read to this special bird. Buddy loves all types of books, but like Maxine, he has a particular fondness for the works of Dr. Seuss.

Do Macaws Make Good Pets?

Macaws like Maxine are amazing and intelligent. But do they make good pets?

Macaws are the largest members of the parrot family. All birds have special needs, and large birds are particularly complicated

to care for. A smaller bird—such as a canary, budgie, or parakeet—may be a better choice, especially for beginning bird owners.

Adopting a parrot or macaw can be a life-long commitment. That's because they live very, very long lives. They are highly social animals and need lots of time and attention.

Birds don't behave like other pets. They're not domesticated like dogs and cats. Even when living with humans, they are wild animals at heart.

Large birds are loud and often destructive. If scared or upset, they may bite. A parrot's beak is especially sharp and powerful. They'll chew on furniture, wires, and other objects. This behavior is part of a bird's natural nest-building tendencies.

If you are thinking about adopting a pet bird, do lots of research. Read about different bird types and what's necessary for their care. Learn about proper bird diet and exercise.

Talk to professionals, such as an avian veterinarian (a vet who specializes in birds). Visit a bird rescue or shelter and talk to the professionals there.

If you decide a bird is the right pet for you, consider getting two! Birds are flock animals.

They do best when living with at least one other bird.

Meet the Paw Pals

 **Meg Harper** is ten years old and has already traveled the world thanks to her father's job as a computer expert. Always being the new kid in school has made Meg a bit shy. At age six, she was diagnosed with epilepsy, a

disorder that causes her to occasionally have seizures. Meg is often accompanied by her service dog, Chance.

Amanda Midori is a few months younger than her cousin Meg, but she's a natural leader. She's a straight-A student with exceptional organizational skills. Amanda lives with her family above their grooming salon, the Wash and Wag.

Drew Bixby is Amanda's next-door neighbor. Younger than the cousins, he shares their love of animals. He also enjoys playing sports and going on outdoor adventures with his scouting troop.

 **Blanca Montez** has been Amanda's friend since kindergarten. Curious and chatty, she is full of questions and always ready to lend a hand.

Chance is a black and white border collie. Abandoned outside the Wash and Wag, Chance was eventually adopted by Meg. Now a trained service animal, Chance helps Meg cope with having epilepsy. He is the Paw Pals' official mascot.